P9-CEA-829

Go Home!

THE TRUE STORY OF JAMES THE CAT

WRITTEN & ILLUSTRATED BY LIBBY PHILLIPS MEGGS

ALBERT WHITMAN & COMPANY • MORTON GROVE, ILLINOIS

Library of Congress Cataloging-in-Publication Data

Meggs, Libby Phillips.
Go home! : the true story of James the cat / by Libby Phillips Meggs.
p.   cm.
Summary: A homeless cat spends several seasons trying to survive
the elements until at last a suburban family adopts him.
ISBN 0-8075-2975-3
[1. Cats Fiction. 2. Lost and found possessions Fiction.] I. Title.
PZ7.M5144Go   2000
[E]—dc21   99-41372
CIP

For Phil, Andrew, Elizabeth,
James, Charlotte, and Emily

Dear Reader,

This is a simple story, but it needs to be told. You may have read about cats who survived a tough city environment. I have, and I've been deeply touched.

This book, James's story, tells the true events that happened to an aging, lost cat, in a peaceful, "safe" neighborhood, where everyone assumed he had a home.

James made us open our eyes a little wider, and he surely made us open our hearts. I hope, when you read about James, the same thing will happen to you.

Libby Phillips Meggs

LOST? FOUND?
...n your lost & found pet ad in this
...olumn ABSOLUTELY FREE! Call
...43-1031 to run your lost or found
...ad in the classifieds for one week.

FOUND CAT—Black male w/white
chest & paws. Wearing flea collar.
Older. Western Henrico county. 74...
9272

REWARD—LOST SHELTIE
Collie) sable colored w...
chest. 33 pds., lost in ...
Wyndom Rds. area. Dog's ...
Mickie. 937-3008 or 417-...

MULTI COLORED T...
SHELL CAT LOST ...
2nd. 2 yrs. old, spa...
humans. Named Mar...
in the 6000 blk. of ...
Ridge. Call 383-98...

09 BUS...
OPPORT...

POSTAL JO...
$14.90/ hr. F...
tion informat...
ext. VA-119...

THE BLACK CAT could
not remember who
had put the collar
around his neck, or when. It
had been buckled on when he
was smaller and younger,
before the long, long time of
being lost. Now the collar was
too tight, and he had trouble
swallowing.

In earlier days he had been
a strong and swift hunter.
These days, he looked for
leftover food by the back
doors of houses where other
cats lived.

One evening at the end of winter, he found the home of Charlotte and Emily. When he looked into their sunroom, the other cats hissed in surprise. The black cat hid in the shadows and watched as Charlotte and Emily's people came to see why they were upset. He listened to the kindness in their voices and liked the gentle way they calmed the tabbies. He stayed the night and all the next day, hidden in the woods behind their house.

When the people came out to their yard, the children cried, "Look at the pretty black cat!"

The woman stooped and held out her hands, calling him.

He came trotting. The woman gently scratched between his ears. It had been so long since anyone had petted him! He sat up and hugged the woman's hand.

"I think he's lost," said the boy.

"No, he's somebody's cat. He's wearing a collar," the girl pointed out.

"But it's awfully tight," their mom observed.

They didn't know how tight it was, how hungry he felt, or how their friendly words and kind hands made him wish he were their cat.

They told him goodnight, and he watched from the edge of the woods. Watched as the lights in their house went out one by one, and long after that, watched the darkened windows.

The world grew warmer. Springtime brought new baby birds and bunnies to the yard. The black cat saw them from the woods.

One afternoon, the people spotted him again at the edge of the yard.

"It's that nice black cat!" called the boy.

But the girl wondered, "What if he eats the baby animals?"

They didn't know he was not fast enough to catch anything.

He made his way to the woman, who patted him, but then said, "You need to Go Home now."

And she squirted the hose at him!

The cat stumbled back to the woods, confused. He did not know where "Home" was. And the only person who had been kind to him had just told him to go there.

Summer came; there was no rain. The cat tried to stay cool as he hid in the woods. There were no puddles where he could get a drink. Even the creek dried up. He watched a turtle walk across dry sand where cool water once had flowed.

He knew what it was like to be hungry all the time, but now he was even more thirsty than hungry.

Then suddenly one night, a huge, horrible storm appeared. Wind screamed, thunder shook the earth, and lightning crackled like white fire. The cat ran for cover as rain beat down in sheets. He found a dry place under the people's shed.

At last the storm left, grumbling and snarling across the sky. The only sound was the dripping of water from the trees.

Water! The cat crept across the lawn to drink from a puddle.

He was almost there when he heard the growl. A monster of a dog flashed his huge teeth in the moonlight. With one leap he had the cat in his jaws. The cat twisted and clawed until the dog dropped him to the ground. Before the dog could snatch him again, the cat slipped under the shed. The dog was too large to follow him there.

The cat listened, terrified, while the dog sniffed and whined around the little building. The dog did not leave until sunrise.

The next day, the cat crawled to the edge of the shed. There stood the kind woman.

"Oh, you poor cat. You've been terribly hurt!"

She saw where the dog had hurt him and how very thin he was. She took off his tight collar. No fur grew where it had cut into his skin.

"You've been lost a long time!" she cried. "If only I had known!"

She picked him up and held him close. He remembered being held before, but how long ago it had been!

The children came out to see the cat.

"Mom, he needs help right now," they said.

"Let's take him to the veterinarian," she replied.

They rode in the car to the veterinarian's office.

The doctor examined the cat carefully, then cleaned his wounds, put medicine on them, and even gave him a shot. Through all of this, the cat was very well-behaved.

"What a good, brave cat he is," the doctor said. "He's lucky you found him."

"I have a feeling *we* are the lucky ones," said the woman. The children agreed.

"These wounds will heal," said the doctor, "but he will always have a hard time walking. He should become a House Cat."

The black cat wondered what a House Cat was.

Back at the house, the children had put a cozy blanket in the sun for the black cat. He had not felt anything so warm and soft since he was a kitten snuggled close to his mother. He loved his toys, too. Being a House Cat was not bad!

Every day he felt stronger. His leg dragged a little, but he soon learned to get around very well. Before long, Charlotte and Emily came to see how friendly and good-natured the cat was.

The family talked. "He's such a wonderful cat. Somebody must be missing him. It isn't right for us to keep him."

So they advertised in the newspaper and with signs around the neighborhood.

But no one came, and no one called.

"Well, we've tried," they said, smiling. "He must be Our Cat now."

Being Their Cat was a good thing. As autumn came, the black cat grew sturdy, frisky, and full of fun.

The family tried lots of names for him:

Merf. Mr. Boots. Boo. Chester. Benjamin. Tommy.

But none of them seemed right. Whenever these names were called, he left the room.

Finally, at Halloween, some trick-or-treaters came to the house.

"James! Hurry up, James!" one little witch cried out to her brother.

The black cat jumped to the windowsill as if he'd heard his name.

The woman saw this. "James," she called. "Are you James?"

He came to her, purring grandly, as if to say, "Yes. I am James, Your Cat from now on."

No harm ever came to James again. Nowadays, he loves to watch the children's aquarium. From the sunroom, he is amused by the backyard birds, bunnies, and chipmunks. When James plays in the yard, someone always goes out and stays with him, to make sure he is safe.

The family cuddles and feeds him. They sing to him and play games with him. In the daytime, James has his blanket downstairs in the sun. At night he sleeps upstairs with the family.

The day is long past when the woman told James to "Go Home."

James purrs as he lies by the fire with Charlotte and Emily while winter's winds cover the world with ice and snow.

"This is where Home is," he thinks, smiling. "My Home."